ttuM

BY

TEDDY JAM

WITH PICTURES BY

HARVEY CHAN

A GROUNDWOOD BOOK

DOUGLAS & McINTYRE

TORONTO VANCOUVER BUFFALO

Groundwood Books/Douglas & McIntyre
720 Bathurst Street, Suite 500, Toronto, Ontario M5S 2R4

Distributed in the USA by Publishers Group West
1700 Fourth Street, Berkeley, CA 94710

We acknowledge the financial support of the Canada Council for the
Arts, the Ontario Arts Council and the Government of Canada
through the Book Publishing Industry Development Program
for our publishing activities.

Canadian Cataloguing in Publication Data
Jam, Teddy
ttuM
"A Groundwood book."
ISBN 0-88899-373-0 (bound) ISBN 0-88899-374-9 (pbk.)
I. Chan, Harvey. II. Title.
PS8569.A427T78 1999   jC813'.54   C99-931255-3
PZ7.J153567Tt 1999

Printed and bound in Canada by Webcom Ltd.

For Honey Jam — TJ
For Mélisan — HC

CHAPTER ONE

It was the last day of school, and Charlotte felt like crying. Not because of her report card. That was being sent in the mail. Not because she would miss her friends. They would all be together in class next year.

Miss Ginn was standing at the front of the classroom. She *was* crying, and now Charlotte began to sniffle.

"Excuse me," Miss Ginn said, making a strange choking sound. This turned into a loud hiccup, and everyone in the class laughed, including Miss Ginn and Charlotte.

"Well, it took all year," said Miss Ginn, "but now you can say you finally made the teacher cry."

Everyone laughed again, although in the middle of the laughs were some loud sobs.

Charlotte sniffed and sighed. Mimi gave her a poke.

"Baby," Mimi said, but her eyes were red.

"My husband was going to come and meet you today, but he had to go to Vancouver to rent us an apartment," Miss Ginn said.

Charlotte was glad she didn't have to meet this husband. If Miss Ginn hadn't got married to a man who was moving to Vancouver, she would have been their teacher again next year. Miss Ginn was the best teacher in the whole school, the best teacher Charlotte had ever had, possibly the best teacher in the world.

When Charlotte was in grade one, she fell and cut her knee in the playground. Miss Ginn picked her up and carried her to the office. While she was fixing Charlotte's knee she gave Charlotte a chocolate bar from her own purse. It was a Milky Way chocolate bar. After that, whenever her father showed her the Milky Way in the sky, Charlotte could taste the chocolate bar and smell Miss Ginn's perfume.

Charlotte and Miss Ginn became friends.

In grade two, Charlotte was in the choir with Miss Ginn.

In grade three, when Miss Ginn was coach of the neighborhood baseball team, Charlotte learned to play baseball.

In grade four, Charlotte walked into her new class and Miss Ginn was at the front desk. The first thing she did was make Charlotte hall monitor.

Now, instead of being Charlotte's teacher in grade five, she was moving to Vancouver.

"Although my husband couldn't come today," Miss Ginn continued, "a very good friend of mine could. Louise Downing is her name. I've known her ever since I went to teacher's college, and by a very wonderful coincidence, she is going to be your teacher next year. She only has one bad habit, which is that she likes to give things away. Everything from cookies to her own brother."

No one laughed. Everyone knew Miss Ginn just said Louise Downing gave things away so they would like her. But they weren't going to be fooled. They liked Miss Ginn better. Some

Fridays Miss Ginn handed out candies so everyone would have a good weekend. On Valentine's Day she sent all the children valentines, to their houses, in envelopes with stamps. And each valentine said something different.

The door opened and a woman limped in with crutches.

"Louise!" said Miss Ginn. "What happened?"

"Look at her leg," Mimi said. Miss Downing's foot and ankle were heavily taped.

"It's wood," a boy whispered, and everyone around him laughed.

Charlotte looked at Miss Downing's face. It was round, like a cookie. Miss Ginn's face was narrow and beautiful, and she had bright blue eyes. Miss Downing wore glasses that hid her eyes. Not only that, but the glasses were taped together at one corner.

"My car had an accident," Miss Downing said. "I had to go to the hospital so they could look at my ankle. They gave me these very nice crutches."

"Are you sure you're all right?"

"I'm fine. I was just in a hurry because I was trying to be on time."

"She was trying to be on time," Charlotte whispered to Mimi, in the voice she used to make fun of people.

"Be nice," Mimi said.

"Why should I? I hate her."

"Hello, everyone," Miss Downing said. "I'm so glad to meet you, even if I am late. And I'm really looking forward to getting to know you all next year."

When Miss Downing talked, Charlotte could see little lipstick stains on her front teeth. Lipstick makes you look cheap, her mother had told her. Miss Downing looked something. She took off her glasses and gave a big lipsticky smile. Then she fell over.

"Down goes Miss Downing," Mimi whispered.

But before Charlotte could say, "That's not nice," Miss Ginn had helped Miss Downing to her feet again, and they were on their way out of the classroom.

CHAPTER TWO

It was the last out of the last inning, and Charlotte was up to bat. She was wearing green satin shorts with a little gold stripe on each side, green socks with a little gold circle at the top, and a green T-shirt with gold printing across the front.

"Come on, Charlotte!" called Mimi.

"Hit it, Charlotte!" called the rest of Charlotte's team.

Charlotte pulled her helmet down over her head. The pitcher was a boy – a skinny, gangly, bucktoothed boy who looked too big to be playing ten-year-old baseball.

"Get her, Spaghetti!" his team yelled. That was what they called him: Spaghetti.

"Come on, Meatball," Charlotte said.

"Did you say Meatball?" asked the catcher.

Charlotte ignored the catcher. If the pitcher was Spaghetti, then he must be throwing meatballs. And Charlotte loved meatballs.

Suddenly she had a strange feeling. This Spaghetti was going to throw her a meatball, and she was going to hit this meatball back over the Spaghetti so hard that Spaghetti would never forget it.

The pitch was coming.

Charlotte had her weight back, the way her father had told her. "Unloading" was what the coach called it when you took your bat off your shoulder and swung. "Time to unload," Mimi and Charlotte now joked to each other as they took off their schoolbags when they got home.

"Time to unload," Charlotte said to herself as she took her bat off her shoulder and started her swing. But this time was different. She must have tripped or something, because her whole body was shooting forward as though it had been fired from a cannon. And the bat seemed to have taken off on its own, like some magic power was inside her and had decided to explode.

WHAM!!!

The bat hit the ball so hard that its ringing noise hurt her ears.

And that was when it happened. The big stupid meatball of a ball exploded all over the infield.

"Run, Charlotte!" screamed her coach.

"Run, Charlotte, run!" Mimi screamed.

"Run, run, Charlotte!" her whole team called.

Charlotte looked toward her father.

"Run!" he shouted.

Charlotte ran.

She ran to first base, where the first baseman tagged her with a little shred of the ball's cover. Then she ran to second base, where the second baseman tagged her with a piece of elastic. Then she ran to third base, where the third baseman just watched her go by on her way to home.

The catcher was waiting for her. In her big catcher's mitt she had as many pieces of the ball as she'd been able to pick up while Charlotte ran around the bases. When Charlotte got home, she slid into the plate. Her green and gold socks dragged in the dust as the catcher tried to tag her. Some of the pieces of ball dropped out of her glove as she did.

"Home run!" screamed Charlotte's coach. "We win!"

"Out at first!" screamed the other coach. "We win!"

Charlotte stood at the plate dusting herself off. Either her team had won because of her or they had lost because of her.

"Take it over!" screamed the other coach. Charlotte picked up the bat. But all the magic that had been in her was gone. She knew that if she hit the ball again, she would just give it a feeble tap, the way she usually did.

"Put the bat down!" screamed Charlotte's coach.

Charlotte looked up at the sky. The clouds that had been threatening all afternoon were turning black.

Suddenly Charlotte felt the magic in her again. "Rain!" Charlotte said.

The rain came pelting down.

"Rain harder!" Charlotte said.

It rained harder.

Charlotte couldn't believe it. Nothing magic had ever happened to her before. This must be her lucky day.

It was raining harder and harder. No one seemed to know what to do. The other team was still picking up pieces of the ball. Their coach looked up at the sky, shook his fists and called out, "Stop raining!"

The rain didn't stop. It got worse. Charlotte's father herded Charlotte and Mimi into the car. The rain was so thick it gushed off the windshield. By the time they arrived home, you could hear it slurping down the drains, as though the street was turning into a river.

CHAPTER THREE

"There it is," Charlotte said as they got out of the car.

"What?" said her father.

"There, across the street."

The rain had plastered her father's hair to his face and he couldn't see. But Charlotte was wearing her baseball cap, and it made a dry space in front of her eyes.

Standing in the narrow gap between two houses was a small black dog. It had a way of opening its mouth so you could see its tiny white teeth and its pink tongue, and its ears had a funny way of flopping. Seeing Charlotte, the dog cocked its head, wagged its tail hopefully and stepped toward them.

"It's the dog," Mimi said. "There's that dog."

A big moving truck was coming down the street. Big waves of water shot out from beneath its wheels. Mimi pointed at the dog, which was now at the sidewalk, ready to cross the street.

Charlotte's mother had opened the door and was standing on the porch. "Hey, kids," she called. "Watch out for the truck."

Charlotte could see everything that was going to happen as though it was a movie. The truck would keep coming. The dog would run in front of it. The truck wouldn't be able to stop. The dog would be sent flying through the air …

"Nooo!" Charlotte screamed. She started running across the street.

"Charlotte!!" screamed her father, and he ran after her.

Charlotte reached for the dog, which was still standing on the sidewalk, its head slightly to one side. She wrapped her arms around it and fell onto the lawn. The dog's fur was wet and smelled like leaves and grass. The grass she fell on was wet and instantly soaked her clothes.

"I thought I was already wet," Charlotte was

thinking, when her father fell on top of her. The three of them lay on the grass as the truck stopped in front of them.

"Hey," called the driver. "That was crazy. Never do that again."

"That's right," said Charlotte's father. "Never do that again."

The truck started up. Charlotte's father rubbed his knee. The dog had crawled out from under Charlotte and was looking at her. Its nose was next to Charlotte's nose.

"I'm sorry," Charlotte said. The dog's nose was black and wet, and its face was covered with black and brown fur. Its eyes were a dark bluey black with black circles in the middle. The rest of its fur was different shades of brown and black, and was plastered to its body by the rain.

Charlotte reached out to touch the dog.

"I wonder what kind of dog it is," she said.

"Some kind of mutt," said her father.

"Mutt?"

"That means different kinds of dogs all mixed together."

"I know," Charlotte said. "But its name isn't Mutt. Mutt? Is your name Mutt?"

The dog backed away.

"You see?" said Charlotte. "It doesn't know that name."

"Mutt," said Mimi. "Come here, Mutt."

The dog backed farther away.

"Instead of coming, it goes," said Charlotte. "It must be a backwards dog. Let's see. Mutt backwards is ttuM. ttuM?"

The dog stopped backing away.

"ttuM! emoC ereH!"

The dog came to Charlotte and put its nose to her face.

"tiS!"

ttuM sat.

"dooG goD," Charlotte said.

She stroked the fur back from the dog's muzzle between its eyes. ttuM felt cold. She put her hand on ttuM's side. ttuM was shivering.

"That's the craziest thing I've ever seen you do," Charlotte's mother said. "Never do that again."

"I already told her," said Charlotte's father.

"Good," said Charlotte's mother. "Did anyone notice that it's raining out?"

"It's called ttuM," Charlotte said.

"It's a she," Mimi said. "And she only understands backwards."

Charlotte's mother helped Charlotte's father up. His pants were torn all down one side.

Suddenly Charlotte had a picture of the truck coming down on her. She could hear the sound of its wheels in the water. She could see ttuM watching as Charlotte ran toward her. Something about the look in ttuM's eyes had made her run faster. Splash, splash, splash her feet had gone. Then suddenly it was as though she was flying.

"ttuM saved my life," Charlotte told Mimi. She hugged the dog, wet and scratchy, until her mother pulled her away.

"You'll get fleas."

The rain was still pouring down on them, as if it was coming out of a big tap. "Come on," Charlotte's mother said, and she took Charlotte's and Mimi's hands to lead them across the street.

"Come on, ttuM," Charlotte said. But the dog didn't move. Charlotte's father had already crossed the street and was waiting for them. Charlotte reached down to take ttuM's collar, but she didn't have one. Charlotte tried to make a little clucking sound between her teeth to attract the dog. It came out "Gssk, gssk." "Gssk, gssk," Charlotte said again. "Come on, ttuM." Her mother was tugging at her.

Charlotte pulled her hand out of her mother's, then lifted ttuM up and started carrying her across the street.

"Charlotte! What are you doing?"

"She saved my life. And she's all wet and she doesn't have a collar. Are we going to let her stay out here and get rained to death as a reward for saving me?"

"Charlotte," her father said in a warning voice.

"I know," Charlotte said. She was carrying ttuM up the steps. "As soon as she's dry and we give her a drink, she can go back to where she belongs. Wherever that is."

When they were in the house, ttuM ran

around excitedly, jumping from Charlotte to Mimi to Charlotte's mother to Charlotte's father.

"Down, you mutt," Charlotte's father said.

"ttuM, please," Charlotte reminded him.

"tiS," Mimi commanded. ttuM sat. "What a dog," Mimi said. "You're so lucky." She gave ttuM a pat and ttuM rolled over on her back and stuck her legs into the air.

Meanwhile, Charlotte's father had brought down towels for the two girls. ttuM scrambled to her feet and followed Charlotte and Mimi into the kitchen.

"It's really raining," Mimi said.

They looked out the back door into the yard. Before the baseball season the yard had been covered with grass. Then Charlotte and Mimi decided to practice sliding into second base because Miss Ginn said good baseball players always got the extra base. Soon there was a small patch of bare ground. Then more practice made the patch larger, and it started to get a little bit dented.

Now second base was a pond filled with water. The rain was jumping on the pond and the wind made little waves. A Popsicle stick came floating across.

"It's funny it started raining that way," Mimi said. "Right when they were arguing. And the way you hit the ball. Wow! I've never seen anyone knock a ball to pieces. Not even on television. How did you do that?"

"I don't know," Charlotte said. "I just had a funny feeling."

CHAPTER FOUR

It was almost suppertime before Charlotte's mother came upstairs to Charlotte's room. Charlotte and Mimi were braiding ribbon necklaces for ttuM.

"Can you believe it? I forgot about her," Charlotte's mother said.

"She's sleeping over," Charlotte said. "She always sleeps over on Saturdays."

"The dog. I forgot to get rid of the dog. Charlotte, go put it outside. Then you girls can help me with the supper. Charlotte, I need you to cut the beans. Mimi, you can make that special salad dressing you showed me last time."

"Come on, ttuM," Charlotte said. "Do you like beans?"

"I love beans," croaked Mimi in a voice that was supposed to sound like a dog, but came out so raspy that Charlotte started to laugh.

"That dog goes outside," Charlotte's mother said.

"She saved my life!"

"Charlotte."

"ttuM doesn't want to go outside. ttuM likes it here."

ttuM was lying on the floor, her mouth slightly open, pink tongue sticking out.

"ttuM needs to go home," Charlotte's mother said. "Somewhere a little girl just like you is wondering where she is. Now why don't you open the front door so she can go."

Charlotte tried to think of who that little girl might be. No one in her class had a dog called ttuM. She was sure of that, because one day everyone in the class had written stories about their pets. Every single kid in the class had a pet — dog, cat, goldfish, hamster — except Charlotte. Mimi had a goldfish *and* a rabbit. The rabbit was called Eleanor. She was twenty-four years old and spent her days eating newspapers. At night she threw up.

In her story about Eleanor, Mimi had said she was the oldest rabbit in the world. Of course, Mimi couldn't really know that. To be sure, she would have to know the age of every rabbit in every country, including rabbits in countries she didn't even know the names of. Mimi had told Charlotte that since she didn't have a pet of her own, Charlotte could borrow her goldfish to write about.

Mimi's goldfish was called Goldie, and it liked to eat snail poo. Charlotte didn't want to write about Goldie. Instead she wrote a story about a mouse who tried to move into her breadbox. "That mouse was the only pet I ever almost had," Charlotte wrote. "And it wasn't even mine."

"I wish I had a mouse," Nicky had said to Charlotte. He had twin golden retrievers called Hercules and Zeus. "What was its name?"

"Squeaky," Charlotte said, although she was just making that up.

"Did it come when you called it?"

"No," Charlotte said. "But it could walk on its hands. Squeaky was a circus mouse. That's why I let her go. She ran away from the circus to stay with us. Then she had to go back and support her poor old mother and father."

"I don't believe you," Nicky said.

"Well," said Charlotte, "if you want I'll sell you a ticket to go see them."

Now Charlotte was kneeling on the floor beside ttuM. "She doesn't even have a collar," Charlotte said. "She doesn't belong to anyone. If we put her outside she'll starve to death."

"She must have left her collar at home," Charlotte's mother said. "She looks like a very well-groomed dog to me."

"That's because she had a bath in the rain and then we brushed her."

"You —"

In fact Charlotte had not planned to say that she and Mimi had brushed ttuM. First they used Charlotte's hairbrush, until it got all clogged. Then they brushed ttuM's teeth with an extra toothbrush they had found in the bathroom.

"Never mind," Charlotte said. "Come on, ttuM."

The dog lay still.

"Her name isn't really ttuM," her mother said. "She has her own name."

"She likes ttuM," Charlotte said.

ttuM lay on the floor, her eyes going back and forth as they talked.

"Look at her," Charlotte said. "She's upset."

"She's someone else's dog," Charlotte's mother said. "I'm going to call the animal shelter and report her missing. Someone must be worried sick."

When they went down for supper, Charlotte's mother said that there had only been an answering machine at the animal shelter. She had left a message describing the dog and giving their phone number.

"At least we can keep her for the weekend," Charlotte said. "At least promise me that."

"We could try to take her in tomorrow," Charlotte's father said.

"Oh, sure, and let her get diseases. That's what

you do for a dog who saved your daughter's life. Thanks a lot."

"You're welcome," Charlotte's father said.

But there was something in his voice that made Charlotte know she'd won. She looked across the table at Mimi. Mimi was putting two slices of tomato on her veggie burger the way she always did. Charlotte took a slice of tomato and put it on her plate.

"You're eating tomato?" her mother asked. Charlotte was famous for never voluntarily eating a vegetable that wasn't a potato or a green bean.

"Just to be healthy," Charlotte said. "Like ttuM. We're both going to be healthy together."

That night, when Charlotte and Mimi went to sleep in the twin beds in Charlotte's room, ttuM lay on the rug between them.

"Do you think you're going to get to keep her?" Mimi asked.

"Well, we don't want her getting sick at the shelter."

"They don't really get sick at shelters," Mimi

said. "If animals all got sick at shelters, they wouldn't have them."

"It was a story," Charlotte said. "Like long division."

"Long division?"

"Yes," Charlotte said. "Long division is just a story. It doesn't really work. I've tried it. It takes hours, and I never get a single right answer. It doesn't work. I think Miss Ginn was just pretending."

"You think she just made it up?"

"Not her. Someone else made it up. And then everyone pretends to believe it. Like if you don't brush your teeth you'll get cavities. Do you ever brush your teeth?"

"Last week I brushed them twice," Mimi said. "My mother came to the bathroom and watched me."

"You don't have any cavities."

"No," said Mimi.

"Me neither. I never brush my teeth. Sometimes I put water on my toothbrush."

"I don't know how to do long division either," Mimi said.

"But you always get the right answer."

"I have a special way. Like say you have thirteen into two zillion. Try that."

"That's impossible. There's no such thing as two zillion."

"I'll give it to myself," Mimi said. "Okay, thirteen into two zillion. Now, I could just write it down the way Miss Ginn showed us and work it out a bit at a time, right?"

"We're supposed to have our lights out."

Mimi giggled. "It doesn't matter. You know what I do? First I close my eyes."

Charlotte could just see them next year. Miss Downing would be crutching around the room watching everyone divide thirteen into two zillion. Everyone would be doing it the right way except for Charlotte, who didn't know how to divide, and Mimi, who would be looking at the ceiling with her eyes closed.

"Okay," Charlotte sighed. "Tell me what you do when you close your eyes."

"First I find a big number and multiply it by thirteen in my head."

Mimi could multiply in her head. Whenever someone ordered pizza Mimi figured out the tip by closing her eyes and looking at the ceiling. Sometimes you could see her sticking out fingers and talking to herself.

"Then what?"

"I get a number that comes close to two zillion," Mimi said. "Closer than thirteen. Then I write it down and what's left over."

"Miss Downing will think you copied it from me," Charlotte said.

"I'll have my eyes closed."

"But you could have looked before."

"You always get the wrong answer."

Charlotte hated long division. She hated when a teacher, even Miss Ginn, stood at the front of the room and explained things. It made the sound of a train going through her head.

"They probably won't have long division next year," Mimi said.

Charlotte knew Mimi was trying to make her feel better. But her stomach felt like a knot inside.

"You're really good at reading," Mimi said. "And finding lost dogs."

"Oh, thanks a lot. You're really good at going to the bathroom." They started laughing. Then ttuM jumped up onto Charlotte's bed, and she felt a bit better.

CHAPTER FIVE

On the ride up to the cottage, Charlotte sat in the back with ttuM. ttuM lay on the seat behind Charlotte's father, her neck stretched out and her head in Charlotte's lap. Every few minutes Charlotte's father asked if ttuM needed to throw up.

"She looks sick," he would say. "If she throws up that's it."

"Don't worry, Henry. If she throws up we'll just clean up with the towel."

"Don't keep talking about it," Charlotte said.

A whole week had passed since they had called the animal shelter, and no one had inquired. Now Charlotte was being allowed to keep ttuM for a while. At least for their time at the cottage.

Before the trip Charlotte's mother took

Charlotte to the pet store. They bought ttuM a collar, an engraved metal tag with her name and telephone number, some puppy dog food and bowls for eating and drinking.

The car was stuffed so full that on the seat under ttuM were several blankets and towels. The top towel was red. ttuM, black and curly on the red towel, looked like some kind of royal dog on a red velvet cushion.

Charlotte's mother had the map. It was spread out over the dashboard and half the windshield. Drawn on it was a red line showing their planned journey from downtown to the cottage on the Lake of Bays.

"Lake of Bays," Charlotte's mother said. "Doesn't it sound wonderful? We're going to spend four weeks on the Lake of Bays. I feel like a little girl again."

"Oh, great," said Charlotte's father. "Now I've got two little girls. So who is going to clean up when ttuM gets sick?"

"You are," Charlotte's mother said calmly. "ttuM's your dog, remember?"

"Not exactly," Charlotte's father said.

When she first noticed that her parents sometimes argued, Charlotte worried that they might get a divorce. Lots of kids in her school lived in two houses. There was a boy in her class called Timmy. He not only lived in two houses, but he had two complete sets of pets — a dog, a cat and a hamster — at each house. One day Mimi said his parents only gave him all those pets so they wouldn't feel bad about taking away his family.

"He has two families now," Charlotte said. "Isn't that better?"

"Then why is he always crying?" Mimi said.

Now, petting the curly black and brown fur on ttuM's head, Charlotte realized she had only seen Timmy cry once, and that was when Mimi whacked him across the shins with a hockey stick. That was the day after Timmy gave Mimi a birthday card that Mimi wouldn't show anyone.

"How long until we turn off?" Charlotte's father asked. "Or maybe we should let the dog out so it can be sick on the side of the road."

Charlotte lifted ttuM's chin and looked into

ttuM's doggy eyes. ttuM's doggy eyes were big. They were blue and white. They looked trustingly up at Charlotte. *I love you,* ttuM's eyes were saying. *I love you, too, ttuM,* Charlotte tried to make her eyes say.

"Her mouth is open," Charlotte's father said. "She's going to bring up."

"ttuM isn't sick," Charlotte said.

ttuM licked Charlotte's hand.

"Maybe she's hungry," Charlotte said.

"Feeding her will definitely make her bring up," Charlotte's father said. He pulled off the road at a little picnic area and they all got out. Charlotte put ttuM on a leash and walked her around. Her father got some water and poured it into ttuM's drinking bowl.

ttuM stuck her face in the bowl and began to slurp at the water. There was something about the sound of ttuM slurping water that Charlotte loved. Also the way her pink tongue worked at the water, scooping it up in little ttuM tonguefuls that she brought to her mouth and nose. ttuM always finished by putting her paw in the bowl, then pushing the bowl over.

Charlotte could tell her father was still thinking about all the bad things ttuM might do.

"Thank you for letting me keep ttuM," she said to him.

"Thank your mother," Charlotte's father said. Then he knelt down and patted ttuM while she pawed at the bowl. When he stood up, he had a big patch of water on his knee, but he didn't seem to mind.

Just after they started driving again, Charlotte saw a car that had a dog with its nose stuck out the window.

"Look at that," she called to her mother. "Can ttuM stick her nose out the window?"

"You're not supposed to put your nose out the window," Charlotte's father said.

"Why not, Henry?" asked Charlotte's mother. "It's so the dog doesn't get sick."

"Someone might knock its nose off by mistake," Charlotte's father said.

"Henry!"

Charlotte knew this meant she could open the window. She let it down a tiny crack. The air came whistling into the car, and the map Charlotte's mother had been holding began to snap and fill up like a sail in a storm. Suddenly it jumped right out of her hands and wrapped itself around Charlotte's father's face.

"Henry, watch where you're going!!"

Charlotte's father pulled the map down. Now it pressed against his chest like a big bib.

"We could have been killed," Charlotte's mother said.

Ahead of them was a big station wagon. Roped onto the top were three bicycles. "I wish I had brought my bicycle," Charlotte was going to say. The two kids in the back seat of the station wagon turned around to look at them. They were both eating giant ice cream cones.

The sight of those big ice cream cones gave Charlotte a funny feeling. She could almost taste the ice cream sliding along her tongue.

"I wish I had an ice cream cone," Charlotte said. As though by a miracle, a store with an ice cream cone sign appeared.

"There it is," Charlotte's mother said at the

same time. It was as though she had been waiting for an ice cream cone, too.

"What?" asked Charlotte's father.

"The turnoff."

Before Charlotte could believe her eyes, they had turned off the highway, gone right past the ice cream store, and were driving down a small paved road. Charlotte's throat was suddenly so dry, so empty of ice cream, that it hurt to swallow.

"AAHHGGGLK," Charlotte said. *"AAHH-HGGGGGLLKKKK."*

"What?"

"AAHHHGGGLLKKKK," she croaked. "Need ice cream. Need ice cream bad. *AAHHHGGGG-LLLLLKKKKKK.*"

ttuM licked her face.

"Did you say ice cream?"

"ecI maerC."

ttuM whined.

"ttuM sdeeN ecI maerC."

Half an hour later Charlotte's shirt was stained with two kinds of ice cream. The top of ttuM's head had little patches of strawberry and chocolate.

Charlotte was just swallowing the last of her cone when they came to a store with a big sign:

FRESH WORMS AND GROCERIES

They stopped at the store to pick up the key to the cottage. Charlotte's parents introduced themselves to the store owners while Charlotte looked around.

There were shelves and shelves of groceries – jars, tins, boxes, even fresh fruit and vegetables – but not a single worm.

"They lied about the worms," Charlotte said to her father when they were outside.

Then she saw them. Lined up on a bench beneath a shady tree was a row of small wooden boxes. She took the lid off one of the boxes. A piece of worm was sticking out of the earth. Charlotte pulled the worm free and offered it to ttuM. ttuM turned around and trotted toward the car.

From the store they followed a last dirt road that came to a big wooden sign with the paint worn off.

"We turn right," Charlotte's mother said.

They went down a grassy lane for a minute or two until it also ended. They were at a cottage that looked like it had been empty and falling down for a hundred years.

CHAPTER SIX

When they walked into the cottage, Charlotte still hadn't seen the lake. She couldn't even see it from the cobwebby screen porch, which was decorated with canoe paddles, fishing nets and stacks of old Archie comics.

The cottage itself had a big kitchen and living room that was all one room. Then there were two bedrooms with a bathroom between. One of the bedrooms was for Charlotte's parents. The other had bunk beds and was for Charlotte and Mimi. Mimi was going to arrive by bus because she had gone to a family wedding.

"Where's the toilet?" called Charlotte's mother.

Charlotte went to look at the bathroom. It had a sink on one side, a shower on the other, and in between was a hole in the floor where the toilet was supposed to be.

"Someone stole the toilet," said Charlotte. She had never heard of someone stealing a toilet before.

"I forgot to tell you," Charlotte's father said. "The owner called last night while you two were walking the dog. The toilet broke a few weeks ago when he was standing on it to change a lightbulb. The new one was supposed to be here last week, but it was late. Now it's coming Tuesday."

"Everyone knows toilets aren't for standing on," Charlotte's mother said.

Charlotte's father opened the pink plastic bathroom curtains. "Meanwhile we use that little place out there." He pointed to the outhouse at the edge of the lawn. It was painted green except for the door, which was red except for the window in the shape of a half moon.

"Looks great," Charlotte's mother said unenthusiastically.

"We're in the country," Charlotte's father said. "When I was a boy – "

" – I know," said Charlotte's mother. "When

you were a boy you had to go to the bathroom in the snow and you only had ice for toilet paper."

"Dorothy!"

Charlotte's mother gave Charlotte's father a little kiss on the cheek. Then she went outside and started toward the outhouse.

Charlotte followed her mother out the door.

Behind the cottage was a wide grassy area that would have been lawn if someone mowed it. It was shaded by a giant oak tree that had a swing hanging from two thick ropes. Charlotte ran to it. She began swinging while ttuM tried to follow her, running back and forth and barking until Charlotte was laughing too hard to swing.

On the other side of the tree was a set of steps with moss and grass between the stones leading down to the water. And at the water was a long dock that stuck out into their own little bay on the Lake of Bays.

As Charlotte walked down the steps, ttuM ran to the end of the dock and began barking again.

When Charlotte caught up to ttuM, she could see what ttuM was barking at. Moving slowly across the mouth of the bay was a canoe. In the canoe was a strange tall figure completely covered in black. Black hat hiding the face, big black shirt, black pants.

Charlotte's mother came down to see what was happening. She waved at the faraway canoeist, and a black-clothed arm waved back.

"He's even wearing gloves," Charlotte said. "It must be some kind of canoe robber."

"Sshh," whispered Charlotte's mother. "Sound carries on the water. Listen to the paddle."

Sure enough, now that ttuM had finally stopped barking, Charlotte could hear the paddle scraping along the side of the canoe with each stroke, then the falling drops of water as the paddle lifted clear of the lake.

When the canoe was out of sight, Charlotte went back to the cottage, where her father was trying to cut the grass.

The mower came from the garage beside the cottage. In there Charlotte's father had also found an old metal barbecue that he dragged out onto the lawn as soon as he had a patch clear.

Charlotte's mother discovered several cloth-covered deck chairs and a big straw hat. She took the hat and one of the chairs down to the dock. Then she lay on the chair and read a book. Charlotte found an inner tube that was miraculously full of air, two girls' bicycles with chains that had rusted and didn't go round, and several more boxes of Archie comics.

After lunch Charlotte covered herself in sunscreen, put on her life jacket and floated around in the inner tube. Her mother lay in her chair again, but instead of her book she read Archie comics. She said she remembered them from when she was a little girl. Kicking her way around the dock, Charlotte decided that when Mimi arrived, they would fix the bicycles and start exploring.

That evening, Charlotte's father made a fire in the barbecue and cooked burgers for everyone — veggie patties for himself and Charlotte, meat burgers for ttuM and Charlotte's mother. By the time they had finished eating, the sun was setting. They went down to sit on the dock. As they did, Charlotte saw the canoe again.

"Hello!" Charlotte's mother called, and again the canoeist raised a hand. ttuM whined as though something was wrong.

Suddenly Charlotte had a strange feeling. It was like the feeling she'd had the time she'd been up to bat and she knew something amazing would happen when she hit the ball.

This time she knew there was something haunted about that person in the canoe. Maybe he was from outer space or somewhere even more strange, but Charlotte was absolutely certain something very peculiar would happen that summer.

CHAPTER SEVEN

The next morning Charlotte woke up to her ear being tickled. Thinking it was a mosquito, she slapped at it. ttuM barked and jumped off the bed.

"Oh, sorry, ttuM. Come back." ttuM looked at her suspiciously. Then Charlotte patted the bed. "yrroS, ttuM. emoC." ttuM jumped on the bed. "I'll tell you what," Charlotte said. "We'll go for a walk. klaW? klaW, ttuM?"

ttuM began wagging her tail.

Outside the sun was up, but not yet over the trees. Even walking from the cottage to the little grassy lane, Charlotte's runners got soaked with dew.

ttuM scampered ahead. The grass was full of buttercups, dandelions and weird purple flowers that Charlotte didn't know the name of. Pale blue butterflies flew along beside her, as though they too wanted to go exploring.

At the corner were some wooden posts with mailboxes. ttuM sniffed around them, her nose twitching and jumping. Then she started running down the lane on the other side of the mailboxes, away from Charlotte's cottage, until she disappeared between some trees.

"ttuM," Charlotte called. "ttuM, emoC."

ttuM reappeared. But instead of running right up to Charlotte, she waited at the corner, black stub tail wagging so furiously that her whole behind was wagging with it.

From the mailboxes led the dirt road that went up to the FRESH WORMS AND GROCERIES. Charlotte was planning to ride there with Mimi, after telling her that she knew a grocery store that mostly sold *worms*.

But ttuM wasn't headed in the worm direction. She had gone down the little lane by the lake.

On Charlotte's cottage side of the mailbox there were no other cottages.

But on this new side, where ttuM wanted to go, Charlotte could see several other cottages through the trees.

Beyond them was the lake.

In the morning sun the lake was bright blue, as though someone had just painted it. Though she hadn't noticed it from her own cottage, she could now see that there was a big island. It was an island that would be perfect for a picnic.

ttuM barked. "yakO," Charlotte finally said. "I'm coming."

Behind each cottage was a car or a van. Shiny in the sunlight, sheltered by trees, these bright clean cars and vans looked as though they had come out of a television commercial.

Then she came to the last cottage. It looked even older than their own. Its roof sagged and rolled and had grass growing out between the wooden shingles. From the very middle of the roof rose a big stone chimney, just perfect for a Hansel and Gretel witch.

This cottage also had a car. Or something that used to be a car. Some huge giant wearing metal boots must have given it a kick and squashed in a door and a fender, broken a window and filled it up with cardboard instead of glass, then turned the radio aerial into a pretzel.

Even ttuM was impressed by this strange wrecked car. She walked around it, sniffing and whining. Then she went to the cottage. Charlotte whispered for her to come back. But ttuM insisted on going up the rickety wooden steps to the door, where she made a weird noise. It was a sort of whine and growl combined. Then she barked.

Charlotte hid behind a tree. "ttuM!!! emoC!!!"

But ttuM wouldn't budge.

Finally Charlotte gathered up her courage. She went to the steps and lifted ttuM in her arms.

Through the screen door she could see what seemed to be a perfectly ordinary kitchen. There was a table, three chairs. On the table was a vase with flowers, and a book spread open. Beside the book was a plate filled with cookies.

Charlotte could smell those cookies.

ttuM whined again.

Charlotte hadn't eaten any breakfast. She wanted those cookies so badly her stomach was beginning to hurt.

She had her hand on the screen door. Just a little push and the door would open. Just a little push and she would walk into the falling-down house of a perfect stranger, a stranger whose car had been kicked in by a giant. Just a little push and she could take one of those perfect stranger's cookies.

They were gingerbread cookies. Charlotte loved gingerbread cookies.

ttuM's tongue was out and she was panting. ttuM loved gingerbread cookies, too.

Charlotte felt as though she was in a dream. She wasn't really walking into this stranger's house to take a cookie. It was a dream she was dreaming. She was dreaming a dream and in the dream she was taking a cookie.

Was there anything wrong with eating a cookie in a dream?

You weren't supposed to steal cookies, but in a dream you could eat any cookie you found, couldn't you?

If you couldn't eat a cookie in your own dream, what cookie could you eat?

Charlotte was just leaning on the door, not exactly opening it but not walking away. That's when she saw, behind the table, the huge black iron stove with its big pipe leading into the stone chimney.

That stove was so big, a little girl or a dog could be stuffed inside and no one would even notice.

Tightening her grip on ttuM, Charlotte ran.

She didn't stop running until she came to the corner with the mailboxes.

There, still holding ttuM, she looked out on the lake and saw the same person she'd seen yesterday. It was the person in the canoe with the dark clothes and the black hat. The paddle was dipping up and down as the canoe skimmed across the water.

Charlotte could see exactly where it was going. The canoe was on its way to the falling-down cottage with the gingerbread cookies and the wrecked car.

"nuR!" she called to ttuM. "nuR!!" And, hanging on to her dog, she ran back to her cottage.

CHAPTER EIGHT

They met Mimi in town at the bus stop. Her luggage was almost bigger than she was. She had a knapsack on her back with a sleeping bag on top. From each hand hung a large shopping bag that dragged on the ground.

"Hi. I brought ttuM a present."

"She's at home," Charlotte said. "ttuM and Mom." She picked up Mimi's shopping bags. One had loaves of bread sticking out. The other was covered with a dishcloth and was almost too heavy to carry.

"Sorry I'm late," Mimi said to Charlotte's father. "A car caught fire on the highway, and the bus had to stop behind it."

"Nothing ever happens here," Charlotte said.

"Except there's a giant or a witch living near our cottage who tried to put a spell on me with gingerbread cookies but I didn't take one."

The bus stop was at a gas station. They crossed with Mimi's things to the little supermarket where Charlotte's father had parked.

That was when Charlotte saw it. It. The bashed-in car. Out here in the bright light it looked even worse than it had at the cottage. It looked as though a giant fist had punched a big dent in the roof.

"There's his car," Charlotte said. "Look at it."

"I forgot the paper," Charlotte's father said. "I'll go back to the supermarket." He gave Charlotte some money and pointed to an ice cream sign down the street. "You and Mimi can get cones. I'll meet you back here. Don't get stolen or run over."

"He always says that," Charlotte said, as she started down the street with Mimi.

"My father always tells me not to get lost. I'm only allowed to go to the corner or the park. He must think I'm pretty dumb."

The sidewalk was crowded with people wearing

sunhats and carrying supplies. There were parents with children in strollers, kids on bicycles, white-haired grandparents wearing plaid cotton shirts and straw hats. Everyone in the whole city seemed to have come up to this little town to spend their vacation.

"There," Mimi said.

"Where?"

"There, in front of the ice cream store. Look."

Charlotte looked. As she did, the crowded side-walk suddenly became empty, as though an unlucky wind had blown everyone away.

"I can't believe it," Charlotte whispered.

Just a few steps away from them, holding a double chocolate ice cream cone, leaning on her crutches and staring straight at them, was none other then Miss Downing.

"Miss Downing!!" Charlotte and Mimi said.

"Hi!" said Miss Downing. "I remember you girls. What a nice surprise."

"What a surprise," Mimi said.

"Isn't it a gorgeous day to get some sun!" said Miss Downing. Every time she spoke she gave a big smile, as though she was announcing how happy she was. She was wearing a white straw hat and white gloves, and her face was as white as her hat and her gloves.

"Very nice," Charlotte said. She tried to make her mouth smile back, and she opened her eyes wide so her smile would look more real.

Mimi didn't say anything. Sometimes it seemed to Charlotte that Mimi forgot to be polite.

"You know what's hard?" asked Miss Downing with a big smile. There was something about Miss Downing's smile and voice that made Charlotte feel as if she was already in Miss Downing's class, being asked a question she couldn't possibly answer.

"What's 672 times 2,688?" Miss Downing would ask the class. Then she would turn to Charlotte before Mimi could whisper her the answer and say, "Charlotte, that's an easy one. Tell us the correct answer." And Charlotte knew she would go red and say, "No, I can't."

Now Charlotte was on the sidewalk, going redder than the reddest sunburn. "No," she said.

Miss Downing put on her biggest smile yet. "What's hard is walking on crutches, wearing gloves and eating an ice cream cone at the same time." With that she bit into the ice cream and held it firmly in her teeth like a dog so she didn't have to use her hand to hold the cone. Then she crutched past them and down the street toward the supermarket.

By the time they'd waited in line and bought their cones, Charlotte's father had joined them. On their way to back to the parking lot, Mimi tried holding her ice cream like Miss Downing. It worked perfectly, except that her cone fell off and then Mimi had to hold her ball of ice cream in her hand while Charlotte ran back to the store for an empty cone.

When they got to the parking lot, it was Charlotte's turn to spot Miss Downing.

"Look," she whispered to Mimi.

Miss Downing was crutching along as a store assistant walked beside her carrying a huge box of groceries. And on top of the huge box was an enormous oversized roasting pan. It was so big that just looking at it made Charlotte close her eyes. And when her eyes were closed, instead of seeing nothing at all, she got a picture of that roasting pan filled with ttuM! Around her neck was a red ribbon, and in her mouth was a ginger-bread cookie.

CHAPTER NINE

When they got home, Charlotte's mother came running out looking so upset that Charlotte had a flash of panic. Then her chest felt as though someone was sitting on it and she couldn't breathe.

"What's wrong?" Mimi asked.

"ttuM's gone," Charlotte's mother said.

Charlotte burst into tears. ttuM gone! She must have drowned. Charlotte ran around the cottage, down toward the lake, still crying but hiccuping at the same time. If she could just find ttuM right away, maybe she could pump the water out of her lungs.

She was lying on the dock when her mother caught up to her. Charlotte was still crying. Her heart was going BAM! BAM! BAM! as she tried to find ttuM in the water.

"Charlotte! ttuM just went for a walk. Everything's okay."

Charlotte rolled over. The sun was so bright that all she could see was a big yellow haze around her mother's head. She sat up, feeling foolish. She was still crying but now it was mostly hiccups. "I thought you meant she was dead."

"I'm sorry, sweetie."

Mimi and her father had now arrived.

"So where is she?" Charlotte said.

"I don't know."

Charlotte's chest began to hurt again.

"ttuM!" she called. "ttuM!"

For a moment Charlotte thought she heard the tinkle of ttuM's dog tags. She was so relieved that she started to cry again.

"Look," Charlotte's father said, "dogs don't drown. ttuM can swim. Remember she swam yesterday? I think she just went out to explore. Why don't we go looking for her? With the four of us, we're bound to find her. Now, Dorothy, where did you last see the dog?"

"I was in the deck chair, up on the lawn in the

shade of the pine tree. ttuM was lying beside me. I must have fallen asleep. When I woke up I didn't see her. I went around the house right away, calling her. That was a minute or two before you arrived. Now let's stop being upset and see if we can find her."

But though they searched all around the cottage and went up and down the road shouting ttuM's name, ttuM could not be found.

With every minute that passed, Charlotte felt three horrible things. One was a growing certainty that she would never see ttuM again. The second was a terrible sadness about the fact that ttuM had disappeared. The third was anger at herself for getting used to ttuM being gone.

"Soon ttuM will have been dead for an hour," Charlotte said. "We're all getting used to ttuM being dead. Pretty soon we'll forget her."

"Charlotte!" exclaimed Charlotte's mother. "That's a terrible thing to say. We are not used to ttuM being dead. And ttuM is not dead. ttuM is a dog."

"Dogs can be dead," Charlotte said.

"What she meant," said Charlotte's father, "is that because ttuM is a dog, ttuM did the doggy thing of going to explore. In a few hours she'll be back all smelly and dirty and you'll be ashamed of yourself for carrying on like this."

"I will not! I'll be proud of myself! I'm not just letting ttuM disappear and pretending it isn't happening!"

"Look," Charlotte's father said, "we'll eat lunch. Then I'll drive up to the worm store and look for ttuM on the way. You and Mimi can make a sign and I'll put it in the store window."

"We could make lots of signs," Mimi said. "We could put them on all the telephone poles."

"And in town, too," said Charlotte. "After all, ttuM's the kind of dog that runs away, I guess. That's how we got her."

"Don't worry," said Mimi. "I got her a present." From her knapsack she pulled a plastic bag. It squeaked when she squeezed it. "It's a surprise. She'll really like it."

"She doesn't even know it's here," Charlotte said. She realized she was beginning to think ttuM might be alive after all. Maybe the dog was out there somewhere eating garbage or wandering around foolishly looking for someone to take care of her. That was the scary thing. She could just get herself into someone else's house the way she'd gotten herself into theirs.

Lunch without ttuM was a sad affair. It would have been sadder except for the treats Mimi's mother had sent with Mimi. Seaweed-coated rice rolls wrapped around sweet vegetables. Sticky buns. And a jar full of very strange fish.

Charlotte's mother passed the fish to Charlotte, who sniffed it and turned away quickly.

"Pickled herring," Charlotte's mother said. "Yum, yum. It was so thoughtful of Maryann to send it."

She always called Mimi's parents Sam and Maryann, although Mimi's parents never called Charlotte's parents Henry and Dorothy. They called them "your mother and father," as though Charlotte might not know they had real names.

"Pickled herring?"

"Yes," said Charlotte's mother. "When

Maryann and I were very pregnant, just before you two were born, we used to have lunch together and eat pickled herring and peanut butter sandwiches."

"My mother must have eaten the most," Mimi said. "That's why I was born a week earlier. I needed to get away from all that pickled herring."

"You used to sit in your high chair and eat it with yogurt," Charlotte's mother said.

Charlotte looked at her mother and her friend. Her eyes were filled with tears, and her throat hurt so much she couldn't speak or swallow. And they were talking about pickled herring and high chairs!

"I still like yogurt," Mimi said.

Charlotte stabbed her fork into her sandwich and left it standing there. Then she took her glass of milk and began pouring it over the bread.

No one noticed until the bread was all soaked and the milk had begun to spread onto her plate.

"Charlotte! What are you doing!"

"You've ruined your sandwich!"

"I miss ttuM."

CHAPTER TEN

When she and Mimi had cleared the table, Charlotte took out her drawing pad and began making a sign for ttuM.

> LOST
> Small black and brown girl dog
> answering to the name ttuM.
> Likes backwards talk.
> SERIOUS REWARD

"Serious reward," Mimi read. "How much is a serious reward?"

"A lot," Charlotte said.

"Your whole allowance?"

"How about a hundred dollars," Charlotte said

to her father. "Isn't that a serious reward?"

"It would be serious for me if I had to pay it."

"Why not? We got ttuM for free. Anyway, don't you love her? What if I got lost? How much would you offer? Ten cents?"

"Charlotte!" said her mother. "Are you on your way to your room?"

"Let's open ttuM's present," Mimi said. She handed the plastic bag to Charlotte.

Charlotte took the bag and reached inside. Out came a rubber figure the size of a giant hot dog but fatter. It was a mailman with a bag over his shoulder.

"You know how ttuM always barks at the mailman," Mimi said. "This way she can really get him. Squeeze it."

Charlotte squeezed the mailman. It squeaked.

"What a mailman," Charlotte said. "Too bad ttuM will never be able to enjoy it."

"She will," Mimi said. "But for ttuM he's not a mailman. He's naM li aM. He's Chinese like me."

"I like him," Charlotte said. "Does he eat chocolate cake?"

"No. But he has to go to the bathroom."

For the first time since the ttuM emergency began, Charlotte remembered about the bathroom. "Does he just want to wash his hands?"

"Not exactly," Mimi said.

Charlotte stood up and led Mimi outside. "Our toilet doesn't work because the man who owns the cottage didn't get it fixed in time. So we have to go there."

She pointed to the little house across the lawn.

"I went in one of those once," Mimi said.

"It's not too bad," Charlotte said. "Just hold your nose and be grateful you get toilet paper instead of ice."

"Thanks," said Mimi. "You keep naM li aM while I go."

When Mimi returned, they went to the front of the cottage and called for ttuM a few times. Then they started walking down the driveway. Suddenly Mimi pointed to the dirt at the edge. There were little marks that could be paw prints.

"ttuM!"

"Look! You can see where she went. All we have to do is follow her tracks."

When they got to the mailboxes at the end of the road that led to the worm store, they found dozens of prints, as though ttuM had walked around and around searching for the right box.

"How do we know it's ttuM?" Charlotte said.

"I don't know. The paws look the right size."

"And they came from the direction of our house," Charlotte said, suddenly sure the prints *did* belong to ttuM. "What happened was my mother was lying there reading. You know how she falls asleep as soon as she starts to read. And ttuM got bored and tried to find us."

"Of course. That's what happened."

"So she comes along here to the mailboxes and starts sniffing around and smells our smell strong because we came here yesterday and put our name on the box. Look."

"Then what did she do?"

"Elementary, my dear Mimi. She must have gone somewhere else."

"But Doctor Charlotte! How could you know that?"

"Elementary, my dear Mimi. She must have

gone somewhere else because she isn't here."

"Brilliant. Absolutely brilliant. She's not here, so she must be somewhere else."

"Exactly."

"Let's look for those paw prints," Mimi said.

But the more they tramped around looking, the more their own footprints filled up the road and made it impossible to see anything else.

"She must have followed the smell of the car toward the worm store," Charlotte said. "She probably walked on the grass for a while and then got on the road."

They started up the road.

"Look at those," said Mimi.

Charlotte went to look where Mimi was pointing. There were huge paw prints. They were the prints of a bear or at least a dog big enough to swallow ttuM in one gulp.

"Poor ttuM," Charlotte said, and her throat started to hurt again.

"ttuM," Mimi said.

"ttuM!" Charlotte called. "ttuM!!!"

And then she heard it. A little metal jangle that

ttuM • *75*

sounded like ttuM's name tag bumping into her collar.

"Over there," said Mimi, just as Charlotte was turning her head.

Suddenly ttuM appeared. She was galloping toward them through the high grass. Between bounds she disappeared into the grass, but with every leap her head came higher and closer. She was running hard the way Charlotte loved to see her run, with her pink tongue sticking out and her floppy ears flopping up and down as though they were wings trying to make ttuM fly.

"ttuM!!" Charlotte called. "ttuM!! Over here!!"

Even as she ran toward ttuM, she tried to figure out where she had come from. But there was nothing to see but a little pine and birch tree forest.

CHAPTER ELEVEN

When they got back to the cabin, Charlotte apologized to her mother and father for being so upset and mean while ttuM was missing. Then she apologized to Mimi for not believing that ttuM was still alive. Then Mimi apologized to Charlotte for not believing that ttuM was dead. Then Charlotte's mother apologized to Charlotte for falling asleep and letting ttuM wander off. Then Charlotte's father apologized to Charlotte for wondering if he should pay a serious reward for ttuM.

To celebrate they ate some ice cream that was melting because the freezer didn't work properly. Then they went down to the lake for a swim.

ttuM loved naM li aM.

She carried him everywhere, dropping him

only so she could pick him up, make him squeak, then shake her head back and forth until the squeaking sound made her run in circles.

On the dock ttuM shook naM li aM so hard that he fell into the water. Luckily he floated. ttuM barked at him, then jumped in after and swam up to him, got him in her mouth, then swam with him to shore.

"Look," said Charlotte, "ttuM's a lifeguard. She saved naM li aM's life. She should get a medal."

ttuM barked. Then she ran to the end of the dock and barked again.

Now Charlotte could see what ttuM was barking at. It was that canoe again. The canoe with the person dressed in black with a wide black hat on top. As ttuM barked, a long black arm with a hand in a black glove came up and waved.

"That's the one," Charlotte said to Mimi. "Out there in the canoe. Maybe it's a ghost dressed in black."

ttuM kept barking until finally Charlotte picked her up and turned so ttuM couldn't see the canoeist.

When they had finished swimming, Charlotte took Mimi up to the garage to show her the bicycles. The garages in the lane behind Charlotte's and Mimi's houses in the city had metal doors with little wheels that slid up toward the ceiling when you opened them. This garage had two doors like a giant cupboard, one opening to each side.

Inside the garage was also like a cupboard – a cupboard into which generations of people had put things, but from which nothing had ever been removed.

The garage didn't have a car. Instead there was a huge wagon with big wooden wheels. Mimi said it must have been used for hay, and there were some bits of straw hanging from the sides. Filling the wagon was a huge pile of cardboard boxes.

"Someone must have been about to move, and they left all their boxes here," said Mimi.

There were the bicycles beside the wagon. Someone had built shelves into the walls of the garage, and those shelves were filled with stacks of yellow newspapers, cardboard boxes, dozens of jars and rusting cans full of nails and screws and cobwebs.

Mimi wriggled past a cobwebby high chair to get at the bicycles. "Let's take these out."

They wheeled the bicycles out from the dusty garage to the lane.

One of the bicycles was red, the other green. Charlotte liked the red one better. It had a little leather tool kit hanging from its back seat. Also, it had its own pump. Charlotte unscrewed a valve and tried to pump up the tire. It was strange to think she was pumping air into a tire that had once belonged to another girl just her size. A girl who would look over from her red bicycle to her sister's green bicycle and think that she was glad she liked her own bicycle better.

When her tires were full she gave the pump to Mimi and opened the tool kit. She found a tin of oil and used it to squirt the rusty chains.

"I like that red bicycle," Mimi said.

"It's mine," Charlotte said.

Mimi turned the green bicycle upside down and made its wheels spin. "It's not fair," Mimi

said. "You have the red bicycle and the dog."

"You have a sister," Charlotte said. "And you can do long division in your head."

"You can't ride long division," Mimi said.

Charlotte knew what she was supposed to do. She was supposed to say, "Mimi, you are my guest. Please take the red bicycle."

Instead she said, "I have ttuM right now. Maybe I'll have to give her back."

Mimi sat down and looked at her hands. Charlotte knew what that meant. Mimi would sit and look at her hands until she got her way. She would look at her hands for a whole week if she had to.

"Mimi, you are my guest," Charlotte said. "Please take the red bicycle."

"Thanks," Mimi said. She jumped up. "But now I like the green one."

Soon they were cruising down the lane. Mimi had found a length of rope in the garage and they had tied it to ttuM's collar. Charlotte and Mimi rode slowly so ttuM could keep up beside them.

They stopped at the mailboxes. "Why don't

we see where ttuM goes from here?" Charlotte said. "We'll know where she ran away to."

But while they stood watching ttuM and waiting to see which direction she was going to take, ttuM stood watching them.

"I give up," Charlotte said. "I know what I'll show you. The strange little place I found yesterday."

They continued down the lane until Charlotte could see the bashed-in car.

Charlotte stopped and got off her bicycle. She held her fingers to her lips and whispered "Sshh" to Mimi.

Untying ttuM from the handlebars, Charlotte put her bike down. She waved Mimi forward.

They crept toward the dented car. ttuM started to whine.

"Quiet," Charlotte whispered. "Quiet." But ttuM kept whining.

"peelS," Mimi said.

ttuM stopped and lay down.

They were hiding behind the car, peering out and spying on the cottage. Charlotte was thinking they could creep forward and she could show

Mimi the inside of the cottage through the screen door.

Then she saw someone coming up from the lake toward the cottage. She started to get that funny feeling she'd been getting that summer. It was the same one she had before she hit the baseball and it broke into a zillion bits. The same one she had when she wanted ice cream. But this time...

"Oh, no!" Charlotte groaned. Mimi grabbed her arm.

It was the tall person in black, the one they'd seen in the canoe. But the tall person in black was swinging forward on crutches.

"It's Miss Downing," Charlotte whispered to Mimi.

"Sshhhh," Mimi said.

Miss Downing's head seemed to turn toward them. Then she crutched up her steps and into her cottage. As her door closed, ttuM whined, but Charlotte and Mimi were already creeping back to their bicycles. Then they rode off at top speed, ttuM panting behind them, until they were back at the cottage.

CHAPTER TWELVE

"I think it's really weird that Miss Downing lives down the road from us," Charlotte said.

"I think your parents invited her on purpose and we're going to have long division lessons all summer."

"Thanks," Charlotte said. "That wasn't very nice."

"Sorry. Pretend I didn't say it."

"yakO."

They were lying in the bunkbeds in Charlotte's cottage bedroom. Charlotte had taken the top one because she knew how to climb down at night. She had practiced climbing down because before Mimi came she had tried the bottom bunk. Looking up at what might be the bottom of

Mimi's mattress, Charlotte decided she didn't like the idea of Mimi falling through and landing on her.

Charlotte's mother opened the door. "Time for sleep."

The two girls didn't say anything.

"I'm glad to see you turned your own light out," Charlotte's mother said. Mimi and Charlotte always turned their own light out on sleepovers. Then they would sneak down to the kitchen to make hot chocolate.

"ttuM is sleeping in the living room," Charlotte's mother said. "When you wake up in the morning, be sure to let her out."

After her mother closed the door, Charlotte lay silently in her bunk. From the outside she could hear funny noises. Then she looked at the ceiling. All she could see on the ceiling was a pale rectangle of light that came in the window from the porch light. Her ceiling was like a piece of sky. It made Charlotte feel like a bird.

"I've always wanted to fly," Charlotte said.

"Me, too," Mimi said.

"If I turned into a bird, I'd fly out the window and up into a tree," Charlotte said.

"I'd fly high in the sky."

"Me, too," Charlotte said. "I'd fly so high you couldn't see me."

Charlotte had her eyes closed. Sleeping up on the top bunk was almost like being in the sky. Almost like sleeping in a cloud.

Then she felt a funny feeling in her stomach, like a bird so high in the sky that it forgot it used to be a girl. A bird so high in the sky that it stretched out its wings and glided from cloud to cloud.

"I have to go to the bathroom," Mimi said.

Charlotte opened her eyes. She couldn't tell if she was still gliding like a bird or if she had been asleep. The porch light had gone off. She looked over the edge of the bunkbed toward the door. There was no yellow stripe of light underneath, which meant that her parents were in bed.

"Will you come with me?" Mimi asked.

"Of course," said Charlotte. She wished the bathroom was inside instead of being the outhouse.

She took her flashlight from under the pillow and turned it on. Then she climbed down from her bunk. She was wearing her white pajamas with gray and red elephants. Mimi was wearing Superwoman PJs that her sister had given her.

Using the flashlight they went through the main part of the cottage and out the kitchen door.

ttuM came with them. She was still carrying naM li aM in her mouth, and it squeaked as she walked.

As soon as they got outside, all the noises Charlotte had half heard from her bedroom were suddenly much louder. There was the wind in the branches of the big pine tree, the slap of waves against the shore, the croaking and peeping and cheeping and chirruping and trilling of millions and millions of frogs and crickets and birds.

Charlotte shone the flashlight until it found the outhouse. It was on an angle, as if it might be falling over.

"Thank you for coming," Mimi said.

"We're not there yet," Charlotte said. With Mimi, she was always the one to go first. So even though it was Mimi who had to go to the bathroom and might end up falling over in the outhouse, Charlotte was the first to step off the deck onto the grass. The grass was so cold and scratchy that she started running toward the outhouse.

"Wait," Mimi called. Holding up her pajama pants, she tiptoed across the grass.

"It hurts my feet," Mimi giggled. ttuM dashed back and forth between the girls.

While Mimi was in the outhouse, Charlotte looked up at the sky. It wasn't like the sky on her bedroom ceiling. It was dark and black and deep. It was the real sky in the middle of the night. There was no moon to be seen, but the sky shone with more stars than she had ever imagined. Across the middle of the sky was a huge mass of stars so crowded that they seemed to be growing out of each other. Those stars were the Milky Way.

Charlotte had never seen the stars so bright and so thick. It was enough to remind her tongue of the chocolate bar Miss Ginn had given her in grade one.

Charlotte shone the flashlight toward the stars. The beam of light went up to the top of the tree, then got lost in the darkness.

Charlotte turned off the light. ttuM was pressed against her legs and shivering, as though she was scared of the dark. When Mimi came out, they stood looking at the sky.

Suddenly, in the middle of the stars, a light came on. A white glow started to move across the sky, leaving a trail of brightness behind it until it flared, then disappeared.

"Shooting star," Mimi said. "My sister says that if two friends see a shooting star together, they will stay friends forever."

Charlotte turned to look at Mimi. Even in the day her eyes were almost black. Now they were like tiny starless skies.

Back in her bunk Charlotte dried her feet on the outside of her blanket.

"Goodnight, Charlotte," Mimi said. On their sleepovers Mimi always said goodnight just before she fell asleep.

"Goodnight, Mimi," Charlotte said.

As Charlotte fell asleep she was a bird again, but this time she was gliding in the darkness, her way lit by shooting stars.

CHAPTER THIRTEEN

The next morning, when Charlotte woke up, the sun had filled her room and she could hear her parents talking and eating breakfast in the kitchen. She leaned over her bunk to look at Mimi. Mimi was lying on her stomach reading a comic.

"ttuM ran away again," Mimi said.

Charlotte had a horrible feeling inside her stomach. But it wasn't as bad as it had been yesterday.

"She's a running-away dog," Mimi said.

Charlotte climbed down from her bunk and opened the bedroom door. Her parents were both dressed and drinking coffee.

"ttuM ran away again," her mother said.

"I know."

"She's a running-away dog," said her father.

"I know."

Charlotte went to the door and called ttuM's name. There was no jangle of collar and tag. She looked across the lawn. There was no ttuM bounding toward her, pink tongue sticking out and ears flopping.

Charlotte felt heavy and sad.

"It's a beautiful day today," her mother said.

Mimi came out of the bedroom. She was still wearing her Superwoman PJs.

"We have to go to town this morning for groceries," Charlotte's father said. "The plumber is coming after lunch to install the toilet. You girls had better eat your breakfast."

"We can't go," Charlotte said. "What if ttuM comes back and we're not here?"

"I could stay," said Charlotte's mother.

"You'll just lose her again. Let Mimi and me stay. We can stay together. You go to town and put up the signs we made yesterday. Put one in the worm store, too."

"I don't know," said Charlotte's father.

"We won't go swimming or anything. We'll just hang around the cottage and go for a bicycle ride."

As soon as her parents had left, Charlotte made Mimi get dressed. Then they walked down the road toward the mailboxes. Charlotte had ttuM's leash, in case they found her.

"ttuM! ttuM! emoC! emoC!" Charlotte called. But no ttuM appeared.

When they got to the mailboxes, Charlotte called ttuM again. For a moment she thought she heard a tiny little sharp bark, ttuM's bark. But when she asked Mimi if she heard it, too, she couldn't hear it anymore, even though Mimi said she might.

They stood in the middle of the sandy road. The sun was hot, and Charlotte wished she'd brought a hat. She could feel herself starting to sweat. She knew that when they got home her face would be red, and her mother would say she should have put on sunscreen.

Then she was sure she heard the bark again. She took a step toward it. Another step. Another.

"I know where she is," Charlotte said. She started walking away from the mailboxes and down the lane toward the cottage where they had seen Miss Downing.

"Do you think she stole her?"

"She has a big oven," Charlotte said. "I was going to show it to you yesterday."

"Dog cake. Yuck."

Charlotte wanted to giggle and cry at the same time. "She probably traps her with food," Charlotte said. "I hate her."

The barking stopped. They crept closer to the cabin.

"The car isn't there," Mimi whispered.

"She must have hidden it," whispered Charlotte. "Maybe she saw us yesterday and knows we discovered her."

Now they were close enough to see the chimney. Charlotte pointed it out to Mimi. "It goes right into that big stove," Charlotte whispered.

"There's smoke coming out."

"Stop," said Charlotte.

She had spoken louder than she meant to. The sound of her voice was so loud that she was afraid Miss Downing would hear her.

ttuM started to bark again. It was a sharp yelp-ing sound, and it was coming from the cabin.

Charlotte couldn't stop herself. "ttuM!" she called, and she ran from behind the tree to the cabin door.

As she ran, ttuM's barking grew louder and faster. But when Charlotte got to the steps, she saw that today, behind the screen door, was another solid door.

She looked back. Mimi was still hiding behind the tree, peering out at her. Charlotte waved her forward. Mimi came out and started walking slowly.

"ttuM!" Charlotte called.

There was a new frenzy of barking.

Charlotte knocked on the door. As ttuM con-tinued to bark, Charlotte wondered if her parents would be angry knowing she had gone to a stranger's house and knocked on the door.

"But it wasn't a stranger," she would say. "It was my next year's teacher."

"How did you know?"

"We spied on her," Charlotte would say. "But

we didn't talk to her because we hate her."

No, she wouldn't say that.

There were no footsteps inside, just ttuM's barking. What if someone did come to the door? Charlotte's heart was pounding inside her chest as though it wanted to knock her over. She knocked again.

Now Mimi was standing beside her.

"ttuM's in there," Mimi said.

"I know."

"But no one's home," Mimi said.

"How do you know?"

"Because no one answered the door when you knocked."

"Maybe they're hiding," Charlotte said.

Mimi sat down beside her.

ttuM had stopped barking. Now Charlotte could hear her panting on the other side of the door. Close enough to reach out and touch, if only the door wasn't in the way.

"Let's get her," said Mimi.

"What do you mean?" asked Charlotte.

"We could go through a window."

ttuM started to whine. Charlotte tried to imagine herself going home without ttuM. *You turned your back on your own dog and walked away because you were afraid*, she would say to herself. She didn't want that.

"We'll try the door," Charlotte said. Before she could ask herself what her parents would think, she opened the screen door, then tried the wooden door.

It wasn't locked.

Charlotte walked into Miss Downing's cottage and ttuM leapt straight into her arms, knocking her over and into Mimi.

The three of them ended up down on the floor. Charlotte and Mimi were laughing while ttuM ran in circles around them, sometimes stopping to leap on top and lick their faces.

"You found each other."

Charlotte looked up. Miss Downing was standing in the doorway, looking down at them. She was wearing her black pants, a black shirt, her wide-brimmed black hat, even black gloves!

Miss Downing crutched into the room while

Charlotte and Mimi scrambled to their feet, brushing off their clothes.

Miss Downing sat down at the table and leaned her crutches against it. She took off her gloves and Charlotte saw that her hands were very, very white.

"Can I offer you girls a cookie? Baked fresh this morning."

Just like yesterday there was a plate of cookies in the middle of the table. Gingerbread cookies. Mimi reached out to take one.

Charlotte had ttuM in her arms. Very slowly, trying not to let Miss Downing see, she snapped the leash on ttuM's collar and backed toward the door.

"nuR!!" Charlotte called out. "nuR!! imiM!! nuR!!" She ran out the door and toward her own cottage. Near the mailboxes she slowed down to let Mimi catch up. She grabbed Mimi's cookie and threw it away.

"It's poison! Don't you understand?" Then she started running again, still clutching ttuM, and didn't stop until she got back to her own cottage and collapsed crying into her mother's arms.

CHAPTER FOURTEEN

"Are you crying, Charlotte? What's wrong?"

Charlotte tried to catch her breath but couldn't.

"You'll never guess who we met," said her mother. "Such a nice woman. What a coincidence! We just ran into her at the worm store when we were putting up the sign."

"We rescued ttuM," Charlotte finally managed to pant.

"Rescued her? What from?"

"From the cottage at other end. She was locked in."

Charlotte let ttuM down on the carpet. Mimi had gone to get herself a glass of water at the sink. She had a certain look on her face, and Charlotte knew that look. It meant a terrible mistake had been made and that they were in trouble.

"Locked in?" said Charlotte's father.

"Not exactly locked. I mean, we heard ttuM barking and then I opened the door and she was trapped inside. Then Miss Downing tried to make Mimi eat a poison cookie and we ran."

"Louise Downing is the one we met," said Charlotte's mother. "Your next year's teacher. It's such a coincidence I can hardly believe it. And she's so nice. And so brave! Do you know that Miss Downing is the one we always see in her canoe? All dressed in black and with the big black hat?"

"That's her," Charlotte said.

"Do you know why she wears black?"

"To scare people?"

"Charlotte! You know better. She's allergic to the sun. Imagine that! But she still comes to her cottage every summer. And you know what? She told me she was afraid she was frightening you and Mimi in her clothes. Imagine the idea that you two could be frightened by someone in a black hat!"

"Right," Charlotte said. "What a joke. Did you also talk about long division?"

"You know, Charlotte, I'm very glad you're going to have a good teacher next year. I was afraid Miss Ginn would be back, and to tell the truth I don't think you were learning very much with her."

"Dorothy!" said Charlotte's father.

"She was the best teacher we've ever had!" Charlotte said. "She always let us do whatever we wanted."

"You know," said Charlotte's mother, "if you don't learn long division now, you never will. Believe me. My mother never learned long division and she was embarrassed about it all her life."

"Dorothy!" said Charlotte's father. "Charlotte should learn long division for her own sake, not because of your mother."

"Mimi doesn't know how to do long division," Charlotte said.

"I always get the right answer," said Mimi. "I just don't know how to do it."

"All that's going to change with Louise," said Charlotte's mother. "Don't worry."

"Yes worry," said Charlotte. "She had my dog trapped in her house."

"ttuM," said Charlotte's mother, and she did look worried. "You know, Charlotte, ttuM wasn't always your dog."

"We found her! She's mine now."

"Yes, Charlotte, she is yours now."

The voice had come from the doorway. As Charlotte looked up she had that funny feeling again.

Miss Downing was standing in the doorway. Charlotte's father hurried to open the door, and Miss Downing crutched into the cottage. As she sat down, ttuM leapt into her lap.

"Why does she like you so much?"

"She used to live with me," said Miss Downing.

"Louise, wouldn't you like a cup of tea or coffee?" asked Charlotte's mother.

"That would be lovely. I brought some cookies we could have with it. I hope you girls like gingerbread cookies."

"Live with you! ttuM was yours?"

"Not exactly," said Miss Downing. "She used to

belong to my brother. And my brother, whom you almost met, has married Miss Ginn and moved to Vancouver with her. They couldn't have a dog in their new Vancouver apartment, so yllaS stayed with me."

"Eelass?" Charlotte asked.

"Sally spelled backwards. She only understands things when you say them backwards. She's a very peculiar dog."

"I know," Charlotte said. "We call her ttuM."

"Tum?"

"No, ttuM. Mutt spelled backwards. My father said she was a mutt when we first saw her."

"I was just joking," Charlotte's father said.

"But with just me in the house, ttuM wasn't happy," Miss Downing said. "She started to run away. I thought she was looking for my brother. So I tied her up, but one day she slipped out of her collar and got away, which is why she didn't have a tag when you found her."

"Isn't that amazing?" said Charlotte's mother.

"Great," said Charlotte. Now she was going to have to give ttuM back to Miss Downing *and* learn long division from her. What a great year. Charlotte *hated* Miss Downing.

"When she came to my cabin today," said Miss Downing, "I knew she must have come from somewhere close by. And I was sure I had seen her barking from a dock, but I didn't know which cottage the dock belonged to. So I decided to put a sign up at the worm store so her family would find her. Then I thought I'd better shut her in my cabin so she wouldn't run away and get lost again. She's a bit of a running-away dog."

Charlotte's mother put the tea on the table. Miss Downing held out the plate of cookies. Mimi took one.

Charlotte looked at the cookies. She would rather starve to death than eat one of Miss Downing's cookies.

"Look," said Miss Downing. "After ttuM ran away I had a long talk with my brother. We decided if ttuM found a family with children, she could stay with them. She would be much happier with children to play with instead of a lonely house with only one grown-up person."

"Mimi doesn't live with me," Charlotte said. "She lives next door."

"What I mean," said Miss Downing, "is that I think ttuM has chosen to live with you."

"ttuM is sitting on your lap," Charlotte said.

"A dog can like more than one person," Miss Downing said. "But ttuM is your dog now. Why don't you call her and see what happens."

Charlotte looked carefully at Miss Downing. She knew this was another nasty trick.

"ttuM. emoC, ttuM."

ttuM jumped off Miss Downing's lap and came to stand beside Charlotte. Her mouth was open and her pink tongue was sticking out. Charlotte put her hand down so ttuM could lick it.

"You see?" said Miss Downing. She held out the cookie plate. "Now, Charlotte, would you like to try one of my cookies?"

"They're good," Mimi said.

Charlotte looked at the plate. Mimi had eaten a cookie and she didn't look sick. Her mother and father had eaten cookies and they didn't look sick.

"Oh, all right," Charlotte said. "I guess I'll try

one." She took a cookie, broke off half and gave it to ttuM. Then she bit into her half. It was sweet and a little bit spicy. It made you wonder what the next bite would be like.

Miss Downing smiled. It was the same funny smile she had the day she arrived in class after her accident. Charlotte suddenly realized Miss Downing was the kind of person things happened to. Just like ttuM was the kind of dog that sometimes ran away. And just like she was the kind of girl who sometimes had strange feelings.

"Tomorrow afternoon we'll have tea," Miss Downing said. "And if it's a nice day wear your bathing suits and bring hats and life jackets. We can go out in the canoe. And have a picnic on the island."

She stood and picked up her crutches. Mimi ran and opened the door for her.

As Miss Downing left the house and started crutching down the lane toward her cottage, Charlotte watched ttuM watch Miss Downing. At first the dog stood with her mouth open, as though she was about to follow. Then, without anyone saying anything, she turned and flopped at Charlotte's feet.

Later that evening, when they were out having a barbecue, Charlotte saw Miss Downing's canoe crossing the bay. As she walked with Mimi and ttuM down to the dock so they could wave to Miss Downing, she had that peculiar feeling again. It was a feeling of being all full inside even though she hadn't eaten. It was a feeling of everything being all one piece: her, the water she'd been swimming in all afternoon, Miss Downing's canoe, the wind that was coming off the lake and into her face, ttuM's tongue licking at her ankle.

"I've got an idea," Mimi said. "Close your eyes and pretend you turned into something. Then I have to guess what you turned into. If I guess right, you jump into the water backwards. If I guess wrong, I jump into the water backwards."

Charlotte closed her eyes. ttuM, she thought.

"ttuM," Mimi said.

Charlotte jumped into the water backwards. When she looked up she could see her hair floating

like weeds toward the surface. ttuM, she thought.
And then she saw a big silvery splash on the
water, and ttuM's legs paddling toward her.

ehT dnE